HÄGAR
SACK TIME

There may be some argument about which European first discovered America—an Italian or a Viking. But now the whole world has discovered that jolly Viking, Hägar the Horrible.

Hägar is back with his entire Viking crew plus Helga, Honi, Hamlet, Lute, Snert and, of course, Lucky Eddie, Hägar's sidekick.

Here's your chance to join the more than 100 million people who "discover" and enjoy Hägar every day, in over 1600 newspapers around the world.

Hägar's creator is Dik Browne, twice winner of the Ruben Award, the National Cartoonist Society's highest honor.

Hägar the Horrible Books

THE HORRIBLE

SACK TIME

BY DIK BROWNE

JOVE BOOKS, NEW YORK

HÄGAR THE HORRIBLE: SACK TIME

A Jove Book / published by arrangement with
King Features Syndicate, Inc.

PRINTING HISTORY
Tempo edition published 1976
Charter edition / October 1986
Jove edition / May 1989

ISBN: 0-515-10082-X

Jove Books are published by The Berkley Publishing Group,
200 Madison Avenue, New York, New York 10016.
The name "JOVE" and the "J" logo
are trademarks belonging to Jove Publications, Inc.

PRINTED IN THE UNITED STATES OF AMERICA

10 9 8 7 6 5 4 3 2 1

9-20
DIK BROWNE

DAD, IF SOMEONE DOES YOU BAD — DO YOU EVER DO THEM GOOD?

ABSOLUTELY!

AND I MEAN *GOOD!!*

PING!

DIK BROWNE
11-2

© King Features Syndicate, Inc., 1973.

THESE CLOTHES ARE FILTHY!

NATURALLY! YOU THREW THEM ALL OVER THE FLOOR LAST NIGHT!

COULDN'T YOU HAVE PICKED THEM UP?

DIK BROWNE 12-10

© King Features Syndicate, Inc., 1973.

NO—YOU WERE IN THEM.